This book belongs to:

....

....

....

For my mum, Jude,
a very wonderful cheerer-upper.

PING!

ARGH!

A BRUBAKER, FORD & FRIENDS BOOK,
an imprint of The Templar Company Limited

First published in the UK simultaneously in hardback and paperback
in 2013 by Templar Publishing, Deepdene Lodge,
Deepdene Avenue, Dorking, Surrey, RH5 4AT, UK

www.templarco.co.uk

Copyright © 2013 by Tor Freeman

First edition

ISBN 978-1-84877-349-3 (hardback)
ISBN 978-1-84877-350-9 (paperback)

Printed in China

SKIIID!

OLIVE
AND THE
BAD
MOOD

TOR FREEMAN

B|F|&|F

BRUBAKER, FORD & FRIENDS

AN IMPRINT OF THE TEMPLAR COMPANY LIMITED

Olive was in a bad mood.

This was **not** a good day.

"Hello Olive!" said Molly. "Do you want to play Dinosaurs with me?"

"No," said Olive. "Dinosaurs are for babies."

"They are not!"
said Molly.

"Hello Olive!" said Matt.
"Do you like my
new hat?"

"No," said Olive.
"It is too big and
floppy. Like
a pancake."

"No it isn't,"
said Matt.

Olive stomped along.
Everything is silly,
she thought to herself.
Look at that silly old can.
Look at that silly old flower!
There was silly old Joe.

"Ho!" said Olive. "You're rubbish with that ball. You couldn't catch a cold."

"Oh yes I could," said Joe.

Oh boy, now Olive was **_really_** in a bad mood.

And look,
here was Ziggy,
getting in
Olive's way!

"PLEASE MOVE!"
said Olive.

"There's no
need to shout,"
said Ziggy.

"Hi Olive,"
said Lola.

Olive pretended
not to hear.
That would
show her.

"Hi Olive!"
Lola called.

"OLIVE?"

Olive kicked
a pebble.
Look at that
silly old –

Oooo! The
sweet shop!
Olive's favourite.

SWEETS

Olive went straight in. She bought herself a bag of Giant Jelly Worms.

Olive walked along chewing a Jelly Worm.
What a lovely sunny day!
Look at that jolly green bush!
Look at those sweet little butterflies!

"And there are all my friends!" cried Olive.

"Hello everyone!" called Olive. "Isn't it a lovely day?"

"WE'RE IN
A BAD MOOD!"
said Olive's friends.

"Well, excuse ME for breathing," said Olive.

"I only came over to see if you wanted one of these delicious sweets."

The friends ate Jelly Worms in the sun.
"See," said Olive. "I don't know why you
were all in such bad moods."

"It was lucky I was here
to cheer you up!"

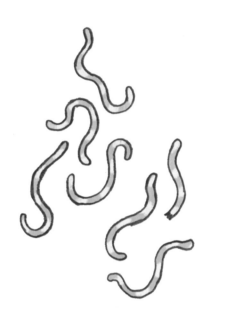